SLIP STREAM

ROBBED!

ANNE CASSIDY

Illustrated by GIULIANO ALOISI

Fiction

STUNT RIDERS
DAVID and HELEN ORME
978 1 4451 1314 2 pb

UNARMED AND DANGEROUS
DAVID and HELEN ORME
978 1 4451 1316 6 pb

WALK INTO DANGER
978 1 4451 1318 0 pb

ROBBED!
ANNE CASSIDY
978 1 4451 1815 4 pb

WOLFHOLD
STEVE BARLOW and STEVE SKIDMORE
978 1 4451 1814 7 pb

WHITE WATER WIPE OUT!
ROGER HURN
978 1 4451 1816 1 pb

Graphic fiction

ALIEN CAGE
JONNY ZUCKER and ...
978 1 4451 1322 7 pb

FUTURE TENSE
JONNY ZUCKER and LEE CARTER
978 1 4451 1320 3 pb

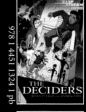
THE DECIDERS
JONNY ZUCKER and ANDREW LEVIE
978 1 4451 1324 1 pb

ASSASSIN CITY
JONNY ZUCKER and PEDRO J COLOMBO
978 1 4451 1803 1 pb

SWORD OF LEGEND
JONNY ZUCKER and COSMO WHITE
978 1 4451 1802 4 pb

SWITCH FACE
JONNY ZUCKER and KEV HOPGOOD
978 1 4451 1804 8 pb

Non-fiction

SUPER ANIMALS
ANNE ROONEY
978 1 4451 1358 6 pb

WORLD'S FASTEST
ANNE ROONEY
978 1 4451 1360 9 pb

GREATEST ROCK BANDS
ANNE ROONEY
978 1 4451 1310 4 hb
978 1 4451 1359 3 pb

SPACE
ANNE ROONEY
978 1 4451 1956 4 hb

DARING ESCAPES
ANNE ROONEY
978 1 4451 1957 1 hb

HOW TO SPEND A BILLION
ANNE ROONEY
978 1 4451 1955 7 hb

CONTENTS

CHAPTER 1
WHERE'S TOMMY?

Lizzie's brother, Tommy, was late.

She called his phone.

No answer.

She asked lots of kids. Nobody had seen Tommy.

Then Lizzie saw his bag.

Tommy's books had been chucked out.

His cash card was not in his wallet.

A boy on a bike stopped.

"I saw Tommy with Big Alex," he said.

"He was going towards the High Street."

Lizzie was worried.

CHAPTER 2
FINDING BIG ALEX

Big Alex was a new boy in their class.

Lizzie was a little bit scared of him.

She saw him on the High Street holding Tommy.

They were walking towards the cash machine.

"He's going to steal from Tommy's cash card," thought Lizzie.

She ran towards him.

"Stop thief!" she yelled.

Lizzie pushed Big Alex away from her brother.

"No, Lizzie!" Tommy said. "It's that boy with the black cap at the cash machine. He stole my phone and my card."

"Oh," said Lizzie.

"And he made me tell him my pin number," said Tommy.

She had been wrong about Big Alex.

He had helped Tommy.

"Quick, we need to get Tommy's stuff back,"

Alex said.

CHAPTER 3

FINDING THE THIEF

They followed the boy to a café.

He went inside.

"What do we do?" Lizzie said.

"I have an idea," Alex said.

Alex went into the café.

"There's a girl outside who is looking for a

cash card," he said.

Nobody said anything.

"She's offering a reward of fifty pounds!" said Alex.

"I found a cash card," the boy said.

CHAPTER 4
GETTING EVEN

The boy held out the cash card.

"Where's my money?" he said.

Alex took a photo of him.

"I'm going to post this photo on line. Unless you

give us the phone and card back!"

The boy ran.

Tommy put his leg out and tripped him up.

They grabbed Tommy's card.

"And the phone!" Alex said, holding his hand out.

Tommy was happy.

Lizzie felt really bad about Alex.

"Sorry," she said. "I blamed the wrong person."

"You could make up for it," said Alex.

"How?" Lizzie asked.

"Never call me Big Alex!" said Alex.

WHITE WATER
WIPE OUT!

ROGER HURN

SLIP STREAM

Rick and Ali are on a school trip.
They go white water rafting and it is brilliant!

Then Rick decides to try the out-of-bounds Hell Hole.
Will Ali be able to save his friend?

LONDON•SYDNEY

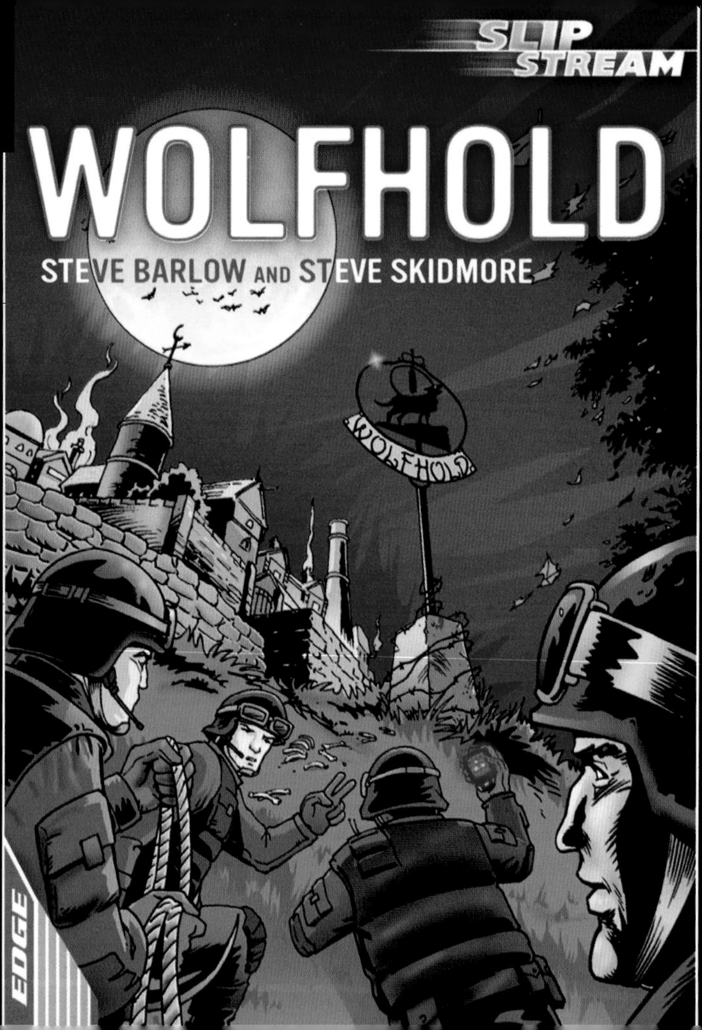
SLIP STREAM
WOLFHOLD
STEVE BARLOW AND STEVE SKIDMORE
WOLFHOLD
EDGE

Tom wakes up in a strange house, in a strange place.
There are no phones, papers or internet, and no way out.

Where is he? And how did he get there? Can the mysterious
Megan help him remember and solve the mystery?

EDGE
FRANKLIN WATTS

LONDON•SYDNEY

About SLIPSTREAM

Slipstream is a series of expertly levelled books designed for pupils who are struggling with reading. Its unique three-strand approach through fiction, graphic fiction and non-fiction gives pupils a rich reading experience that will accelerate their progress and close the reading gap.

At the heart of every Slipstream fiction book is a great story. Easily accessible words and phrases ensure that pupils both decode and comprehend, and the high interest stories really engage older struggling readers.

Whether you're using Slipstream Level 1 for Guided Reading or as an independent read, here are some suggestions:

1. Make each reading session successful. Talk about the text before the pupil starts reading. Introduce any unfamiliar vocabulary.

2. Encourage the pupil to talk about the book using a range of open questions. For example, have they misjudged someone?

3. Discuss the differences between reading fiction, graphic fiction and non-fiction. What do they prefer?

Slipstream Level 1 photocopiable **WORKBOOK** ISBN: 978 1 4451 1798 0 available – download free sample worksheets from: www.franklinwatts.co.uk

For guidance, SLIPSTREAM Level 1 – Robbed! has been approximately measured to:

National Curriculum Level: 2c
Reading Age: 7.0–7.6
Book Band: Turquoise

ATOS: 1.6*
Guided Reading Level: H
Lexile® Measure (confirmed): 250L

*Please check actual Accelerated Reader™ book level and quiz availability at www.arbookfind.co.uk